A BOOK FOR KIDS

This edition published 2025
by Living Book Press
Copyright © Living Book Press, 2025

ISBN: 978-1-76153-299-3 (hardcover)
         978-1-76153-300-6 (softcover)

First published in 1921.

A catalogue record for this
book is available from the
National Library of Australia

A Book for Kids

by

C. J. DENNIS

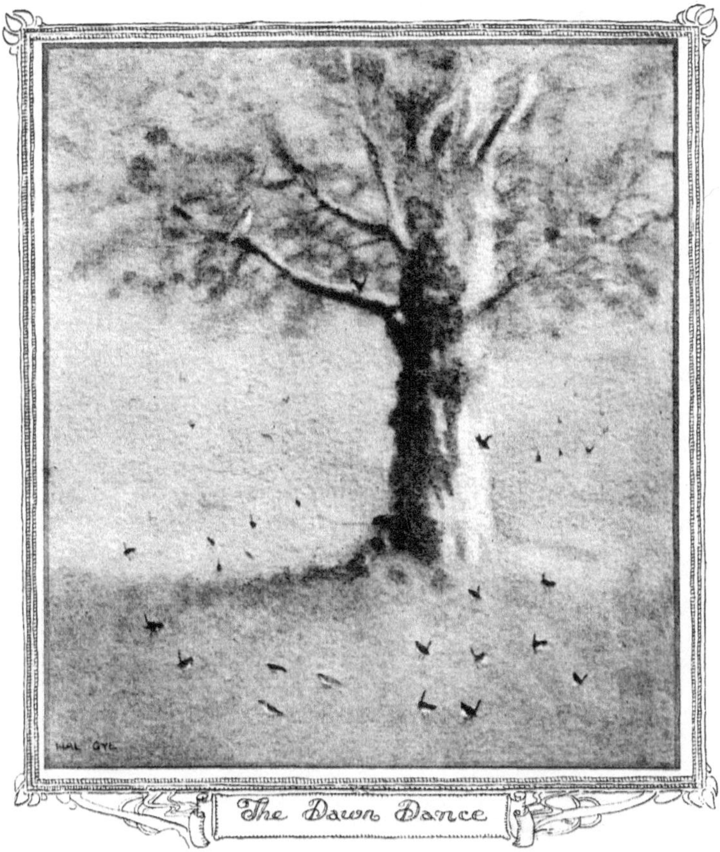

LIVING BOOK PRESS

Contents

A very charming gentleman, as old as old could be,
Stared a while, and glared a while, and then he said to me:
"Read your books, and heed your books, and put your books away,
For you will surely need your books upon a later day."
And then he wheezed and then he sneezed, and gave me such a look.
And he said, "Mark—ME—boy! Be careful of your book."

A very charming gentleman, indeed,
   he seemed to be.
He heaved a sigh and wiped his eye,
   and then he said to me:
"Take your books and make your
   books companions—never toys;
For they who so forsake their books
   grow into gawky boys."
I don't know who he was. Do you? he
   snuffled at the end;
And he said, "Mark—ME—boy! Your
   book should be your friend."

DEDICATION

To all good children over four
  And under four-and-eighty
Be you not over-prone to pore
  On matters grave and weighty.
Mayhap you'll find within this book
  Some touch of Youth's rare clowning,
If you will condescend to look
  And not descend to frowning.

The mind of one small boy may hold
  Odd fancies and inviting,
To guide a hand unsure and old
  That moves, these days, to writing.
For hair once bright, in days of yore,
  Grows grey (or somewhat slaty),
And now, alas, he's over four,
  Though under four-and-eighty.

THE BAKER

I'd like to be a baker, and come when morning breaks,
Calling out, "Beeay-ko!" (that's the sound he makes)—
Riding in a rattle-cart that jogs and jolts and shakes,
Selling all the sweetest things a baker ever bakes;
Currant-buns and brandy-snaps, pastry all in flakes;
But I wouldn't be a baker if...
I couldn't eat the cakes.
Would you?

THE DAWN DANCE

What do you think I saw to-day when I arose at dawn?
Blue Wrens and Yellow-tails dancing on the lawn!
Bobbing here, and bowing there, gossiping away,
And how I wished that you were there to see the merry
  play!

But you were snug abed, my boy, blankets to your chin,
Nor dreamed of dancing birds without or sunbeams
  dancing in.
Grey Thrush, he piped the tune for them. I peeped out
  through the glass
Between the window curtains, and I saw them on the
  grass—

Merry little fairy folk, dancing up and down,
Blue bonnet, yellow skirt, cloaks of grey and brown,
Underneath the wattle-tree, silver in the dawn,
Blue Wrens and Yellow-tails dancing on the lawn.

CUPPACUMALONGA

'Rover, rover, cattle-drover, where go you to-day?'
I go to Cuppacumalonga, fifty miles away;
    Over plains where Summer rains have sung a song of glee,
    Over hills where laughing rills go seeking for the sea,
I go to Cuppacumalonga, to my brother Bill.
    Then come along, ah, come along!
      Ah, come to Cuppacumalonga!
      Come to Cuppacumalonga Hill!

'Rover, rover, cattle-drover, how do you get there?'
For twenty miles I amble on upon my pony mare,
    They walk awhile and talk awhile to country men I know,
    Then up to ride a mile beside a team that travels slow,
And last to Cuppacumalonga, riding with a will.
    Then come along, ah, come along!
    Ah, come to Cuppacumalonga!
      Come to Cuppacumalonga Hill!

'Rover, rover, cattle-drover, what do you do then?'
I camp beneath a kurrajong with three good cattle-men;
  Then off away at break of day, with strong hands on the
    reins,
  To laugh and sing while mustering the cattle on the
    plains—
For up to Cuppacumalonga life is jolly still.
    Then come along, ah, come along!
      Ah, come to Cuppacumalonga!
        Come to Cuppacumalonga Hill!

'Rover, rover, cattle-drover, how may I go too?'
I'll saddle up my creamy colt and he shall carry you—
  My creamy colt who will not bolt, who does not shy nor
    kick—
  We'll pack the load and take the road and travel very quick.
And if the day brings work or play we'll meet it with a will.
    So Hi for Cuppacumalonga!
      Come Along, ah, come along!
        Ah, come to Cuppacumalonga Hill!

THE SWAGMAN

Oh, he was old and he was spare;
His bushy whiskers and his hair
Were all fussed up and very grey
He said he'd come a long, long way
And had a long, long way to go.
Each boot was broken at the toe,
And he'd a swag upon his back.
His billy-can, as black as black,
Was just the thing for making tea
At picnics, so it seemed to me.

'Twas hard to earn a bite of bread,
He told me. Then he shook his head,
And all the little corks that hung
Around his hat-brim danced and swung
And bobbed about his face; and when
I laughed he made them dance again.
He said they were for keeping flies—
"The pesky varmints"—from his eyes.
He called me "Codger"... "Now you see
The best days of your life," said he.
"But days will come to bend your back,
And, when they come, keep off the track.
Keep off, young codger, if you can."
He seemed a funny sort of man.

He told me that he wanted work,
But jobs were scarce this side of Bourke,
And he supposed he'd have to go
Another fifty mile or so.
"Nigh all my life the track I've walked,"

He said. I liked the way he talked.
And oh, the places he had seen!
I don't know where he had not been—
On every road, in every town,
All through the country, up and down.
"Young codger, shun the track," he said.
And put his hand upon my head.
I noticed, then, that his old eyes
Were very blue and very wise.
"Ay, once I was a little lad,"
He said, and seemed to grow quite sad.

I sometimes think: When I'm a man,
I'll get a good black billy-can
And hang some corks around my hat,
And lead a jolly life like that.

THE ANT EXPLORER

Once a little sugar ant made up his mind to roam—
To fare away far away, far away from home.
He had eaten all his breakfast, and he had his ma's consent
To see what he should chance to see and here's the way he
    went—
Up and down a fern frond, round and round a stone,
Down a gloomy gully where he loathed to be alone,
Up a mighty mountain range, seven inches high,
Through the fearful forest grass that nearly hid the sky,
Out along a bracken bridge, bending in the moss,
Till he reached a dreadful desert that was feet and feet
    across.
'Twas a dry, deserted desert, and a trackless land to tread,
He wished that he was home again and tucked-up tight in bed.
His little legs were wobbly, his strength was nearly spent,
And so he turned around again and here's the way he went—
Back away from desert lands feet and feet across,
Back along the bracken bridge bending in the moss,
Through the fearful forest grass shutting out the sky,
Up a mighty mountain range seven inches high,
Down a gloomy gully, where he loathed to be alone,
Up and down a fern frond and round and round a stone.
A dreary ant, a weary ant, resolved no more to roam,
He staggered up the garden path and popped back home.

RIDING SONG

Flippity-flop! Flippity-flop!
Here comes the butcher to bring us a chop
    Cantering, cantering down the wide street
    On his little bay mare with the funny white feet;
Cantering, cantering out to the farm,
Stripes on his apron and basket on arm.
    Run to the window and tell him to stop—
    Flippity-flop! Flippity-flop!

THE FUNNY HATTER

Harry was a funny man, Harry was a hatter;
He ate his lunch at breakfast time and said it didn't matter.
  He made a pot of melon jam and put it on a shelf,
  For he was fond of sugar things and living by himself.
He built a fire of bracken and a blue-gum log,
And he sat all night beside it with his big—black—dog.

THE POSTMAN

I'd like to be a postman, and walk along the street,
Calling out, "Good Morning, Sir," to gentlemen I meet,
Ringing every door-bell all along my beat,
In my cap and uniform so very nice and neat.
Perhaps I'd have a parasol in case of rain or heat;
But I wouldn't be a postman if...
The walking hurt my feet.
Would you?

THE TRAVELLER

As I rode in to Burrumbeet,
I met a man with funny feet;
And, when I paused to ask him why
His feet were strange, he rolled his eye
And said the rain would spoil the wheat;
So I rode on to Burrumbeet.

As I rode in to Beetaloo,
I met a man whose nose was blue;
And when I asked him how he got
A nose like that, he answered, "What
Do bullocks mean when they say 'Moo'?"
So I rode on to Beetaloo.

As I rode in to Ballarat,
I met a man who wore no hat;
And, when I said he might take cold,
He cried, "The hills are quite as old
As yonder plains, but not so flat."
So I rode on to Ballarat.

As I rode in to Gundagai,
I met a man and passed him by
Without a nod, without a word.
He turned, and said he'd never heard
Or seen a man so wise as I.
But I rode on to Gundagai.

As I rode homeward, full of doubt,
I met a stranger riding out:
A foolish man he seemed to me;
But, "Nay, I am yourself," said he,
"Just as you were when you rode out."
So I rode homeward, free of doubt.

OUR STREET

In our street, the main street
　　Running thro' the town,
You see a lot of busy folk
　　Going up and down:

　　　　Bag men and basket men,
　　　　　Men with loads of hay,
　　　　Buying things and selling things
　　　　　And carting things away.

　　　　　　The butcher is a funny man,
　　　　　　　He calls me Dandy Dick;
　　　　　　The baker is a cross man,
　　　　　　　I think he's often sick;

The fruiterer's a nice man,
　　He gives me apples, too;
The grocer says, "Good morning, boy,
　　What can I do for you?"

　　　　Of all the men in our street
　　　　　I like the cobbler best,
　　　　Tapping, tapping at his last
　　　　　Without a minute's rest;

　　　　　　Talking all the time he taps,
　　　　　　　Driving in the nails,
　　　　　　Smiling with his old grey eyes—
　　　　　　　(Hush)... telling fairy tales.

THE LITTLE RED HOUSE

CHAPTER ONE

Very few grown-up people understand houses. Only children understand them properly, and, if I understand them just a little, it is because I knew Sym. Sym and his wife, Emily Ann, lived in the Little Red House. It was built on a rather big mountain, and there were no other houses near it. At one time, long ago, the mountain had been covered all over with a great forest; but men had cut the trees down, all but one big Blue-gum, which grew near the Little Red House. The Blue-gum and the Little Red House were great friends, and often had long talks together. The Blue-gum was a very old tree—over a hundred years old—and he was proud of it, and often used to tell of the time, long ago, when blackfellows hunted 'possums in his branches. That was before the white men came to the mountain, and before there were any houses near it.

Once upon a time I put a verse about the mountain and the Little

Red House into a book of rhymes which I wrote for grown ups. I don't think they thought much about it. Very likely they said, "Oh, it's just a house on a hill," and then forgot it, because they were too busy about other things.

This is the rhyme:

A great mother mountain, and kindly is she,
Who nurses young rivers and sends them to sea.
And, nestled high up on her sheltering lap,
Is a little red house, with a little straw cap
That bears a blue feather of smoke, curling high,
And a bunch of red roses cocked over one eye.

I have tried here to draw the Little Red House for you as well as I can; and it isn't my fault if it happens to look just a little like somebody's face. I can't help it, can I? if the stones of the door-step look something like teeth, or if the climbing roses make the windows look like a funny pair of spectacles. And if Emily Ann will hang big fluffy bobs on the window blinds for tassels, and if they swing about in the breeze like moving eyes, well, I am not to blame, am I? It just happens. The only thing I am sorry for is that I couldn't get the big Blue-gum into the picture. Of course, I could have drawn it quite easily, but it was too big.

Sym and Emily Ann were fond of the Little Red House, and you may be sure the Little Red House was fond of them—he was their home. The only thing that bothered him was that they were sometimes away from home, and then he was miserable, like all empty houses.

Now, Sym was a tinker—a travelling tinker. He would do a little gardening and farming at home for a while, and then go off about the country for a few days, mending people's pots and pans and kettles. Usually Sym left Emily Ann at home to keep the Little Red House company, but now and then Emily Ann went with Sym for a trip, and then the Little Red House was very sad indeed.

One morning, just as the sun was peeping over the edge of the world, the big Blue-gum woke up and stretched his limbs and waited for the Little Red House to say "Good morning." The Blue-gum always waited for the greeting because he was the older, and he liked to have proper respect shown to him by young folk, but the Little Red House didn't say a word.

The big Blue-gum waited and waited; but the Little Red House wouldn't speak.

After a while the Blue-gum said rather crossly, "You seem to be out of sorts this morning."

But the Little Red House wouldn't say a word.

"You certainly do seem as if you had a pain somewhere," said the Blue-gum. "And you look funny. You ought to see yourself!"

"Indeed?" snapped the Little Red House, raising his eyebrows just as a puff of wind went by. "I can't always be playing the fool, like some people."

"I've lived on this mountain, tree and sapling, for over a hundred years," replied the big Blue-gum very severely, "and never before have I been treated with such disrespect. When trees become houses they seem to lose their manners."

"Forgive me," cried the Little Red House. "I didn't mean to be rude. I was just listening. There are things going on inside me that I don't like."

"I hope they aren't ill-treating you," said the Blue-gum.

"They are going to leave me!" sighed the Little Red House. "And they are laughing quite happily, as if they were glad about it. There's a nice thing for you!—Going to leave me, and laughing about it!"

"But perhaps you are wrong," said the big Blue-gum, who was not so hard-hearted as he seemed.

"I always know," moaned the Little Red House. "I can't be mistaken. Sym was singing his Tinker's song this morning long

before the sun was up. And then I heard him tell Emily Ann not to forget her umbrella. That means that she is going; and the little dog is going, and I shall be all alone."

"Well," answered the Blue-gum rather stiffly, "you still have me for company."

"I know," sighed the Little Red House. "Don't think I'm ungrateful. But, when they both go away, I shan't be really and truly a home again until they come back—just an empty house; and it makes me miserable. How would YOU like to be an empty house?"

"Some day I might be," replied the Blue-gum, "if I don't grow too old. There is some fine timber in me yet."

Suddenly there was a great clattering and stamping inside the Little House, and Sym began to sing his Tinker's song.

"Kettles and pans! Kettles and pans!
All the broad earth is the tinkering man's—
The green leafy lane or the fields are his home,
The road or the river, where'er he may roam.
He roves for a living and rests where he can.
Then bring out your kettle! ho! kettle or pan!"

There's a nice thing for you!" said the Little Red House bitterly. "What kind of a song do you call that? Any old place is good enough for his home, and I am just nothing!"

"Oh, that's only his way of putting it," answered the Blue-gum kindly.

"He doesn't really mean it, you know; he wants a change, that's all."

But the Little Red House wouldn't say a word.

"It looks a good deal like rain this morning, doesn't it?" said the Blue-gum cheerfully, trying to change the subject.

But the Little Red House wouldn't say a word.

Very soon Sym and Emily Ann, carrying bundles, came out of the Little Red House, laughing and talking; and Sym locked the door.

"Now for a jolly trip!" shouted Sym, as he picked up his firepot and soldering-irons.

But all at once Emily Ann ceased laughing and looked back wistfully at the Little Red House.

"After all I'm sorry to leave our little home," she said. "See how sad it looks!"

"Hurry on!" cried Sym, who was all eagerness for the trip. Then he, too, looked back. "Why, you forgot to draw down the blinds," he said.

"No, I didn't forget," answered Emily Ann, "but I think it a shame to blindfold the Little Red House while we are away. I just left the blinds up so that he could see things. Good-bye, little home," she called. And the Little Red House felt just the least bit comforted to think that Emily Ann was sorry to leave him. Then she went off down the winding path with Sym; and Sym began to shout his Tinker's Song again.

The Little Red House watched them go down the mountain.

21

Away they went: through the gate, past the black stump, round by the bracken patch and over the bridge, across the potato paddock, through the sliprails—getting smaller and smaller—past the sign-post, down by the big rocks—getting smaller and smaller—under the tree-ferns, out on to the stony flat, across the red road, until they were just two tiny specks away down in the valley. Then they went through a white gate, round a turn, and the high scrub hid them.

Had you been able to see the Little Red House just at that moment, you would have been sure he was going to cry—he looked so miserable and so lonely.

"Cheer up!" said the big Blue-gum.

But the Little Red House couldn't say a word.

Presently the big Blue-gum groaned loudly.

"Oo! Ah! Ah! Golly!" groaned the Blue-gum in a strange voice.

"I beg your pardon? said the Little Red House.

"Oh, I have a nasty sharp pain in my side," said the Blue-gum. "I do hope and trust it isn't white-ants. It would be simply horrible, if it were. Fancy getting white-ants at my time of life! Here I have lived on this mountain, tree and sapling, for over a hundred years; and to think those nasty, white, flabby little things should get me at last is horrible—horrible!"

"I am sorry," said the Little Red House. "I'm afraid I've been very selfish, too. I was forgetting that everyone has troubles of his own; but I hope it isn't so bad as you fear."

"It is bad enough," groaned the Blue-gum. "Ow! There it is again. I'm afraid it IS white-ants. I can feel the wretched little things nipping."

But the Little Red House hardly heard him. He was thinking again of his own troubles.

So they stood all through that day, saying very little to each other. Rabbits came and played about the Little Red House, and lizards ran over his door-step, and once a big wallaby went flopping right past the front gate. But the Little Red House paid no attention. He was too busy thinking of his loneliness.

Birds came and perched in the branches of the big Blue-gum, and chattered and sang to him, trying to tell him the news of other trees on distant mountains. But the big Blue-gum took no notice. He was too busy thinking about white-ants.

So the sun sank low behind the Little House, and the shadow of the tall Blue-gum began to creep down the mountain and get longer and longer.

Just as it was growing dark, the big Blue-gum said suddenly, "It certainly looks more like rain than ever. The heavy clouds have been gathering all day, and we shall get it properly to-night."

But the rain did not come that night, nor the next day, nor for two days and nights. And all this while the Little Red House and the Big Blue-gum remained silent and miserable—one through loneliness, the other through white-ants.

But on the evening of the third day the big Blue-gum said, "The rain will come to-night for certain. I know by the feel of the air."

"Let it come!" said the Little Red House. "I don't care. I couldn't be more miserable than I am."

Just as he said that, one great rain-drop fell right on the middle of his roof—Plop!

"It's coming already," cried the Blue-gum, "and it's going to pour."

Then three more big drops fell—Plop! Plop! Plop!

"I have never in my life seen such big rain-drops," said the Blue-gum.

"I've lived on this mountain, tree and sapling, for—"

But—Crash! came rain before he could finish; and in two seconds everything was sopping wet. The noise of it was deafening,

"Why, it's a cloud-burst!" shouted the Blue-gum. "Half of my leaves have been stripped off already." Then he peered through the rain and the dark to see how the Little Red House was taking it. "Why, what's the matter with your face?" he cried. "You look awful."

"I'm crying!" sobbed the Little Red House. "That's all—just crying. "Can't you see the tears?"

"Nonsense!" said the Blue-gum. "Those are not tears. It's just the rain-water running off your window-sills."

"I tell you I'm crying!" wailed the Little Red House. "I'm crying bitterly. I should know, shouldn't I? I'm shivering and crying because I'm cold and lonely and miserable."

"Oh, very well," agreed the Blue-gum. "You are crying. But if this rain doesn't stop soon, you'll cry the front path away. It certainly is wet."

Very late that night the rain eased a little and then stopped altogether. The tears ceased to run from the eyes of the Little Red House, and they now came only in drops, slower and slower, falling into the great pool by the front door.

"It's a hard world!" sobbed the Little Red House, squeezing out another tear.

"Listen!" cried the Big Blue-gum. "Do you hear THAT?"

From far away on the distant ranges came a dull, moaning sound. As they listened it grew louder, and right in the middle of of it came another sound—Thump!

"That's wind," said the Blue-gum; "and a big wind, too."

"Let it come!" sighed the Little Red House. "I couldn't be more miserable than I am."

As he spoke, the moaning grew louder, and there were three or four quite big thumps one after another.

"What's that thumping?" asked the little House.

"Those are my poor brothers," answered the big Blue-gum very sadly,

"Those are trees going down before the big wind. The birds were bringing me messages from those poor fellows quite lately; and now I shall never hear from them again. It's very sad."

"I never thought the wind could blow down big trees," said the Little House.

"No tree knows when his time will come," the big Blue-gum answered gravely. "I've had some very narrow escapes in my time, as tree and sapling on this mountain."

The Little Red House was very quiet and thoughtful for a long time after that. Then he asked suddenly, "Which way do you think you would fall if you did fall?"

But the big Blue-gum said that he couldn't tell. It depended on the wind, and he might fall any way.

"Not on me!" cried the Little House.

The Blue-gum said that he didn't know; but he hoped not.

"If you DID fall on me," said the Little Red House, "I suppose it would hurt me."

The Blue-gum said it certainly would, and there would be very little left but splinters and glass.

"Then don't! Please don't," yelled the Little Red House.

But before they could say another word the great wind struck them with a roar. It tossed the roses about so that the eyebrows of the Little House seemed to be twitching horribly; and it swayed the big Blue-gum this way and that till he appeared to be fighting for his very life. It picked up the fallen leaves and twigs, and even small stones, and hurled them down the mountain in a cloud.

In the midst of all the uproar the Little House heard the Blue-gum calling to him.

"As long as I've lived upon this mountain, tree and sapling," he shouted, "I've never known such a wind. I'm not so young as I used to be, and I fear that my end has come."

"Be brave! Oh, be brave!" implored the Little Red House. "Don't let him blow you down. I should be so sorry to lose you, What are you grunting for?"

"I'm not grunting," answered the Blue-gym in a pained voice. "Those are my roots giving way, one by one. I can't stand much more of this.

Look out!"

The Little Red House looked up, and what he saw terrified him. The big Blue-gum, in the clutch of the wind, was bent right

DON'T FALL ON ME!

over him, so that the top branches seemed to be just above his roof; and the great tree appeared to be falling, falling, helplessly.

"Don't fall on me!" shrieked the Little Red House. "Oh, don't fall on me; because, if you do, you know you'll squash me! I don't want to be squashed!"

But the big Blue-gum said, "There is just one little root holding now. If that gives way we are both done for."

"Be brave! Oh, be brave!" shrieked the Little Red House.

Then slowly, very slowly, the big Blue-gum began to straighten up again, away from the Little Red House.

"I have stood upon this mountain, tree and sapling, for over a hundred years," he said when he had recovered; "but if it blows like that again, it is the end of me."

But it did not blow like that again; though the wind howled and shrieked all that day as if it was very angry and disappointed that it could not blow down the big Blue-gum.

Then, towards evening, the wind fell; the heavy clouds went away beyond the edge of the sky, and all became very calm and peaceful.

The birds came from their hiding places and sat in the branches of the Blue-gum and chattered away to him, until he began to feel quite cheerful once more, in spite of his trouble. And when a certain little Tree-creeper—a very wise bird—came and had a long, serious talk with the Blue-gum, he became very much interested indeed and quite happy.

But the Little Red House was miserable still; and the beauty of the evening didn't cheer him up one bit.

"Ah, well," said the Blue-gum, when the darkness came to the mountain, "I am going to have a good sleep tonight. I'm a match still for old Daddy Wind, in spite of all his noise and bluster. And there are ways of dealing with white-ants, too. I've lived upon this mountain, tree and sapling, for—"

But as he was talking he fell fast asleep.

The Little Red House did not sleep. How could he, with his

eyes wide open? So he just stood there all night staring before him, lonely and wretched. And when an owl came and sat in the tree and began to call, "Mopoke," the Little Red House told him rudely to stop his silly noise and clear out. That will just show you how very miserable he was.

It was quite late next morning when the Blue-gum awoke. He stretched his big limbs, and began to wonder what he might say to comfort the Little Red House. But when the Blue-gum looked down, he saw that the Little Red House was smiling all over his face.

"Well, now!" cried the big Blue-gum cheerfully. "That's the kind of face I like to see in the morning! So you've decided to be sensible and forget your loneliness?"

But the Little Red House didn't say a word. He just went on smiling. Then the big Blue-gum began to get uneasy.

"I do hope your troubles haven't turned you silly," he said. "You haven't lost your senses, have you?"

SMILING ALL OVER HIS FACE

"I?" cried the Little Red House. "Why, look down the valley! See who's coming!"

Down, far down, the valley, just coming through the white gate, were two figures that looked like tiny specks. And much nearer was another speck, which was certainly a little dog.

"It's them—I mean those are they!" shouted the Little Red House happily. "Sym and Emily Ann! And here comes our little dog."

"Well, you certainly have sharp eyes," replied the Blue-gum. "But I suppose I'm getting old—over a hundred years, you know."

The two figures were through the white gate now, and had crossed the red road out on to the stony flat—getting bigger and bigger as they came; and the smile on the Little Red House seemed to grow broader and broader. On they came, under the tree-ferns, up by the big rocks, past the sign-post. And now the Little Red House could hear Sym singing his Tinker's song.

But it was not quite the same song this time:

> "Kettles and pans! Ho, kettles and pans!
> Where's there a home like the tinkering man's?
> Weary of wandering, home is the place—
> The Little Red House with the smile on his face—
> Weary and hungry, my Emily Ann.
> Then put on the kettle! Ho, put on the pan!"

"Now THAT is the sort of song I DO like," said the Little Red House, as he watched them coming up the mountain.

On they came, growing bigger and bigger—through the sliprails, across the potato paddock, over the bridge, round by the bracken-patch, past the black stump, through the gate, and here they were, right at the front door.

"Oh, I AM glad to be home again," cried Emily Ann. "And do look at the Little House. He seems to be smiling."

"Of course he is smiling," answered Sym; "but he has a very dirty face."

"The storm did that," said Emily Ann. "Now hurry and get

the fire alight, and I'll put the kettle on." And they went inside laughing and singing, while the little dog flew round the house, barking for dear life, and pretending he was very busy seeing everything was in order.

"Now I suppose you're happy," said the big Blue-gum to the Little Red House.

"Happy?" cried the Little House. "Of course I am. Why, I'm a home again!" But suddenly he remembered that his own happiness had made him forget all about his old friend's troubles; and he tried his best to look serious, as he said: "But what about YOU? Are the white-ants still troubling you?"

"Ah!" replied the Blue-gum. "Don't let that worry you. Yesterday I had a talk with the doctor—Doctor Tree-creeper, you know—a very clever little bird he is, and he knows all about white-ants. He examined me thoroughly all over. He says that they have hardly got under my skin yet, and he will have them all out in a couple of days. So THAT'S all right."

"Well, I am glad," shouted the Little Red House. "Now we are ALL happy!"

Then Sym got the fire started, and the smoke curled up, and the Little House had his gay blue feather once again. Sym began to sing his Tinker's Song louder than ever, and Emily Ann, who was getting the meal ready, joined in and sang too. Very soon the kettle also began to sing, and, when the pan heard that HE began to sing. Then Doctor Tree-creeper arrived to attend to the white-ants, and, as he walked round the trunk of the big Blue-gum, tapping it just like a doctor, HE began to sing. And two Kookaburras, who were sitting on the fence, were so tickled with it all, that they laughed and laughed till they made everyone else laugh with them.

"This is quite like old times," laughed the big Blue-gum. "Are you contented now?"

"Am I contented?" cried the Little Red House. "Am I contented? Well, what would you think?"

And then—well, most ordinary grown-up folk would tell you that just then Emily Ann drew down one of the front blinds. But all the big Blue-gum knew, and all you and I know, is that the Little Red House winked.

And when I saw him last, his smile was as broad as ever, and he was still winking.

THE PIEMAN

I'd like to be a pieman, and ring a little bell,
Calling out, "Hot pies! Hot pies to sell!"
Apple-pies and Meat-pies, Cherry-pies as well,
Lots and lots and lots of pies—more than you can tell.
Big, rich Pork-pies! Oh, the lovely smell!
    But I wouldn't be a pieman if...
        I wasn't very well.

            Would you?

THE TRIANTIWONTIGONGOLOPE

There's a very funny insect that you do not often spy,
And it isn't quite a spider, and it isn't quite a fly;
It is something like a beetle, and a little like a bee,
But nothing like a wooly grub that climbs upon a tree.
Its name is quite a hard one, but you'll learn it soon, I hope.
So try:
   Tri-
      Tri-anti-wonti-
         Triantiwontigongolope.

It lives on weeds and wattle-gum, and has a funny face;
Its appetite is hearty, and its manners a disgrace.
When first you come upon it, it will give you quite a scare,
But when you look for it again, you find it isn't there.
And unless you call it softly it will stay away and mope.
So try:
   Tri-
      Tri-anti-wonti-
         Triantiwontigongolope.

It trembles if you tickle it or tread upon its toes;
It is not an early riser, but it has a snubbish nose.
If you snear at it, or scold it, it will scuttle off in shame,
But it purrs and purrs quite proudly if you call it by its name,
And offer it some sandwiches of sealing-wax and soap.
So try:
   Tri-
      Tri-anti-wonti-
         Triantiwontigongolope.

But of course you haven't seen it; and I truthfully confess
That I haven't seen it either, and I don't know its address.
For there isn't such an insect, though there really might have been
If the trees and grass were purple, and the sky was bottle green.
It's just a little joke of mine, which you'll forgive, I hope.
Oh, try!
   Tri-

      Tri-anti-wonti-

         Triantiwontigongolope.

BIRD SONG

There are many birds—but, Hush!
Hear the carol of Grey Thrush!
  He's my favoured bird among the forest singers.
With his modest coat of grey
And his charming, friendly way,
  He is head and chief of all good-fortune bringers.

I dislike Bell-magpie slightly,
Though he's very neat and sprightly,
  And to humour he has certain solid claims.
But at theft he has no match,
For he raids my cabbage patch,
  Then he sits upon a post and calls me names.

I deplore the Butcher-bird,
For no sweeter song is heard
  Than his chanting in the autumn and the spring.
But he hunts his weaker cousins,
And he butchers them in dozens—
  And I wonder that he has the heart to sing.

THE CIRCUS

(repeated on next spread)

Hey, there! Hoop-la! the circus is in town!
Have you seen the elephant? Have you seen the clown?
Have you seen the dappled horse gallop round the ring?
Have you seen the acrobats on the dizzy swing?
Have you seen the tumbling men tumble up and down?
Hoop-la! Hoop-la! the circus is in town!

Hey, there! Hoop-la! Here's the circus troupe!
Here's the educated dog, jumping through the hoop.
See the lady Blondin with the parasol and fan,
The lad upon the ladder and the india-rubber man.
See the joyful juggler and the boy who loops the loop.
Hey! Hey! Hey! Hey! Here's the circus troupe!

THE CIRCUS
Hey, there! Hoop-la! the
circus is in town!
Have you seen the elephant?
Have you seen the clown?
Have you seen the dappled
horse gallop round the
ring?
Have you seen the acrobats
on the dizzy swing?
Have you seen the tumbling
men tumble up and
down?
Hoop-la! Hoop-la! the
circus is in town!

Hey, there! Hoop-la! Here's
the circus troupe!
Here's the educated dog,
jumping through the hoop.
See the lady Blondin with the
parasol and fan,
The lad upon the ladder and
the india-rubber man.
See the joyful juggler and the
boy who loops the loop.
Hey! Hey! Hey! Hey! Here's
the circus troupe!

YOU AND I

They say the eagle is a bird
    That sees some splendid sights
When he soars high into the sky
    Upon his dizzy flights:
He sees the ground for miles around
    Our house, and Billy Johnson's;
But we cannot be eagles, for
    That would, of course, be nonsense.

But you and I, some summer day,
    Providing we're allowed,
Will go up in an aeroplane
    And sail right through a cloud.

But, if they say we may not go,
    We'll stay upon the ground
With other things that have no wings,
    And watch them walk around.

They say the bottom of the sea
    Is beautiful to view;
They say the fish, whene'er they wish,
    Can sail and see it, too;
The shining pearls, the coral curls,
    The sharks, the squids, the schnappers,
And fish with fins (though not in tins)
    And fish with funny flappers.

But you and I, some sunny day,
    When weather's in condition,
Will go there in a submarine,
    Providing we've permission.
But if they say we may not go
    We must respect their wishes;
And you and I will just keep dry
    Because we are not fishes.

The earth is quite a jolly place,
    And we don't care for flying;
And things that creep down in the deep
    Are sometimes rather trying.
So, if they'll grant a holiday
    Or even only half,
We'll lie upon some grassy place,
    And think of things, and laugh.

GOING TO SCHOOL

Did you see them pass to-day, Billy, Kate and Robin,
All astride upon the back of old grey Dobbin?
Jigging, jogging off to school, down the dusty track—
What must Dobbin think of it—three upon his back?
Robin at the bridle-rein, in the middle Kate,
Billy holding on behind, his legs out straight.

Now they're coming back from school, jig, jog, jig.
See them at the corner where the gums grow big;
Dobbin flicking off the flies and blinking at the sun—
Having three upon his back he thinks is splendid fun:
Robin at the bridle-rein, in the middle Kate,
Little Billy up behind, his legs out straight.

HIST!

Hist!...... Hark!
The night is very dark,
And we've to go a mile or so
Across the Possum Park.

Step...... light,
Keeping to the right;
If we delay, and lose our way,
We'll be out half the night.
The clouds are low and gloomy. Oh!
It's just begun to mist!
We haven't any overcoats
And—Hist!...... Hist!

(Mo...... poke!)
Who was that that spoke?
This is not a fitting spot
To make a silly joke.

Dear...... me!
A mopoke in a tree!
It jarred me so, I didn't know
Whatever it could be.
But come along; creep along;
Soon we shall be missed.
They'll get a scare and wonder where
We—Hush!...... Hist!

Ssh!...... Soft!
I've told you oft and oft
We should not stray so far away
Without a moon aloft.

Oo!...... Scat!
Goodness! What was that?
Upon my word, it's quite absurd,
It's only just a cat.
But come along; haste along;
Soon we'll have to rush,
Or we'll be late and find the gate
Is—Hist!...... Hush!

(Kok!...... Korrock!)
Oh! I've had a shock!
I hope and trust it's only just
A frog behind a rock.

Shoo!...... Shoo!
We've had enough of you;
Scaring folk just for a joke
Is not the thing to do.
But come along, slip along—
Isn't it a lark
Just to roam so far from home
On—Hist!...... Hark!

Look!...... See!
Shining through the tree,
The window-light is glowing bright
To welcome you and me.

Shout!...... Shout!
There's someone round about,
And through the door I see some more
And supper all laid out.
Now, run! Run! Run!
Oh, we've had such splendid fun—
Through the park in the dark,
As brave as anyone.

Laughed, we did, and chaffed, we did,
And whistled all the way,
And we're home again! Home again!
Hip...... Hooray!

BIRD SONG

I am friendly with the sparrow
Though his mind is rather narrow
   And his manners—well, the less we say the better.
But as day begins to peep,
When I hear his cheery "Cheep"
   I am ready to admit I am his debtor.

I delight in red-browed finches
And all birds of scanty inches.
   Willie wagtail is a pleasant bird, and coy.
All the babblers, chats and wrens,
Tits and robins, and their hens,
   Are my very special friends, and bring me joy.

THE MUSIC OF YOUR VOICE

A vase upon the mantelpiece,
  A ship upon the sea,
A goat upon a mountain-top
  Are much the same to me;
But when you mention melon jam,
  Or picnics by the creek,
Or apple pies, or pantomimes,
  I love to hear you speak.

The date of Magna Charta or
  The doings of the Dutch,
Or capes, or towns, or verbs, or nouns
  Do not excite me much;
But when you mention motor rides—
  Down by the sea for choice
Or chasing games, or chocolates,
  I love to hear your voice.

THE BOY WHO RODE INTO THE SUNSET

CHAPTER ONE

Once upon a time—it was not so very long ago, either—a little boy, named Neville, lived with his people in a house which was almost in the country. That is to say, it was just at the edge of the city; and at the back of the house was a rather large hill, which was quite bald.

Neville, who was fond of playing by himself, would often wander to the top of the bald hill; and if he stood right on top of it and looked one way, toward the East, he could see right over the city, with all its tall buildings and domes and spires and smoking chimneys. But looking the other way, to the West, he could see for miles over the beautiful country, with its green fields and orchards and white roads and little farm houses.

One evening Neville was playing alone on the top of the hill when he noticed that one of the very finest sunsets he had ever seen was just coming on. The sky in the West, away over the broad country lands, was filled with little clouds of all sorts and shapes, and they were just beginning to take on the most wonderful colours.

Neville had often before amused himself with watching clouds and the strange shapes into which they changed themselves—sometimes like great mountain ranges, sometimes like sea-waves, and very often like elephants and lions and seals and all manner of interesting things of that sort. But never before had he been able to make out so many animal shapes in the clouds. The sky was almost as good as a Zoo. There were kangaroos and elephants and a hen with chickens and wallabies and rabbits and a funny man with large ears and all sorts of other peculiar shapes.

The sun was sinking behind a distant range of hills, where a golden light shone out as if through a gateway. It was so much like a great golden gateway that Neville fell to wondering what might be found on the other side of it.

Suddenly, right in the middle of all the coloured clouds, he saw one little cloud which was perfectly white, and, as he watched it, he noticed that it seemed to be shaped like a small horse. A very small horse it seemed at that distance; but, as Neville gazed, it grew bigger and bigger, just as if it were coming toward him very fast, and he was almost certain he could see its legs moving.

That startled him a little, and so he rubbed his eyes to make sure that they were not playing him tricks.

When he looked again he was more startled than ever; for the little white cloud was no longer a cloud, but a little white horse in real earnest. Besides, it had just left the sky and was galloping down the mountain range which he could see away in the West.

In two minutes it had left the range, and was coming across the fields towards him, jumping the fences, dodging under the trees, and racing across the plain with its white mane and tail tossing as it came. It seemed to be making straight for him.

He was not really frightened—you must not think that about him—but he was just beginning to wonder if it were not nearly time to go home to dinner, when he noticed that the white horse had stopped, just at the foot of the bald hill. It was looking up at him, tossing its head and pawing the ground—the most beautiful white horse that he had ever seen, even in a circus. Then it appeared to get over its excitement and began to trot quietly up the hill toward him.

I do not think anyone would have blamed Neville if he had decided then to go home to dinner at once. But he was rather a brave boy, and he was certainly very curious, so he just stood still and waited.

And here is where the most wonderful part of the story begins. The white horse trotted up to Neville and spoke to him. That would surprise most people; and Neville was certainly as much surprised as anyone else would have been.

"What are you frightened of?" asked the white horse in a loud voice.

Now, Neville WAS just a little frightened by this time; but he was not going to show it, so he just said, "Who's frightened?"

"*YOU'RE* frightened," said the white horse, louder than ever. "You're only a timid little boy. I thought when I saw you in the distance that you were one of the plucky ones; but I was mistaken. You're just a little cowardly-custard."

"You'd better be careful who you're talking to," said Neville, suddenly losing his fear. (Little boys do not always talk good grammar; otherwise he would have said "whom" not "who.") He hated to be called a "cowardly-custard." "You'd better be careful, or I'll give you a bang!"

"Ah ha!" cried the white horse. "Very brave all at once, aren't you? All the same, you're afraid to come near and stroke me."

"But I don't want to stroke you," said Neville.

"I thought not," replied the white horse. "I thought not, the moment I got close to you. You're one of the frightened ones, and I've been wasting my time."

"Who's frightened?" said Neville again.

"You asked that before," replied the white horse, "and I told you. If you're not frightened, come along and stroke me. There's nothing to be afraid of."

So Neville walked right up to the white horse and stroked his shoulder. And at once he felt that he had been foolish to hold back. For of all the smooth, soft, silky coats he had ever stroked, that of the white horse was certainly the smoothest, and the softest, and the silkiest. He felt that he could go on stroking it for hours.

CHAPTER TWO

"There now," said the white horse in a voice as soft and silky as his coat. "There was nothing to be afraid of, was there? And I think that perhaps I was mistaken about you. I rather think you might be one of those daring boys that one reads about in stories. What about jumping on my back for a little ride?"

Neville ceased to stroke the white horse and drew back a little.

"I'm afraid they'll be expecting me home for dinner," he said. "I'm very pleased indeed to have met you." Neville was always a polite little boy.

"The very thing!" cried the white horse. "Jump on my back and I'll take you home. You liked stroking me, didn't you? Well that's nothing to the ride you will enjoy—simply nothing. Why, all the boldest riders in the world would give their ears just for one little ride on my back. Now then! One, two, three, and up you go!"

Then before Neville quite knew what he was doing, he made a little run and leapt up astride of the white horse.

"I live just over there," said Neville, pointing towards his home.

But before he could say "knife", or even "scissors" (supposing he had wished to say either of these words), the white horse laughed a nasty hollow laugh, sprang upwards from the ground, and was soaring through the air toward the dying sunset, right away from home and dinner.

Neville clung on tightly, for he was so high above the earth that to fall off would mean the end of him. And far beneath him he saw the green fields and the white road, which now seemed like a mere thread.

"That's not fair! Whoa back! Whoa back!" he shouted to the white horse; but the white horse made no reply. Indeed, he seemed suddenly not so much like a white horse as like a white cloud shaped like a horse, and Neville saw that he no longer sat upon the horse's silky coat, but upon something soft and downy like a white fleece, and it was slightly damp. Then he knew that he was riding upon a cloud; and, as it was quite absurd to go on talking to a cloud, he ceased to cry out. He just sat tight and wondered what would happen next.

He was high over a farm-house now: one that he used to see from the bald hill. He knew it by the tall pine-trees that grew round it; and down in the farm-yard he saw a man with a bucket going out to feed the calves. Neville called loudly to him, but the man did not even look up. Now he was far beyond that farm-house and above an orchard, where he saw the fruit-trees standing in straight rows; and a few seconds later the mountain range was beneath him, and Neville knew that the cloud that looked like a horse was making straight for the golden gateway, which was now glowing dully in a grey sky. He was riding into the sunset.

Swiftly as the wind that drove it, the Cloud Horse drifted over the mountain range. There was a sudden glow of golden light all about him, and then a flash of colour so wonderful that Neville could not bear to look. He closed his eyes, and, as he did so, he felt that the Cloud Horse had come to a halt at last.

So Neville sat upon the cloud, not daring to open his eyes for quite a long time. When at last he did look again he almost fainted with the wonder of it. He was inside the sunset.

But scarcely had he begun to enjoy the wonderful sight, when he was startled by the sound of a funny, shrill little voice close by his side. Looking down, he saw a strange little man, no taller than a walking-stick, and dressed from top to toe in golden-yellow clothes. "My stars!" said the wee yellow man. "How did YOU manage to get in here? Don't you know this is private?"

"I'm very sorry," said Neville, "but I couldn't help it. The Cloud Horse brought me, you know."

"Ah!" said the wee yellow man. "He tricked you, did he? He's much too playful, that Cloud Horse; and, I must say, he's put you in a pretty fix."

"Excuse me," said Neville, "but do you mind telling me who you are?"

"I?" cried the little yellow man. "Why, I'm the Last Sunbeam, of course. I thought you knew that. My job, you know, is to shut up the show when the sunset is over. And it's pretty hard work,

I can tell you, because I've got to keep on doing it all round the earth every few minutes or so. And it gets very tiresome at times. Would you believe it? I've never seen a dawn or a bright mid-day in all my life—just sunsets all the time. Sunsets for breakfast, sunsets for dinner, sunsets for supper. And if I make the tiniest little slip, the head scene-shifter is down on me like a ton of bricks."

"Goodness me!" said Neville. "I didn't know you had scene-shifters here." Neville had been to see pantomimes, and therefore knew what a scene-shifter was.

"Then how do you think we shift the scenes?" cried the wee yellow man rather crossly. Then he suddenly became very busy about nothing, as he whispered, "Look out! Here's the head scene-shifter coming now."

Looking back, Neville saw, coming towards them, a man with very large ears. He was not a nice-looking man, and he was extremely like the cloud man that Neville had sometimes seen in the sky when he went to look at the sunset from the bald hill.

"Now then! Now then!" roared the man with the large ears. "Move yourself there, Goldie! We shut up the show here in a few minutes, and open at once on the next range. See that you have that curtain down on time."

"Certainly, sir," replied the little yellow man very humbly.

Then the man with the large ears noticed Neville for the first time. He frowned darkly, and his big ears seemed to flap with annoyance.

"Who is this on our Cloud Horse?" he roared in his great angry voice.

"Just a little boy," said the yellow man—for Neville was far too frightened to speak. "Just a little boy that the Cloud Horse has been playing tricks on. I think he'd like to be getting home—just over by the bald hill, if you don't mind, sir."

"Certainly not!" shouted the man with the large ears. "The Cloud Horse is not to go out there again to-night, nor the silly little boy either. I'm not going to have the sunset upset by any such silly nonsense. You mind what I say and attend to your work." And, without another glance at Neville, the man with the large ears strode off to arrange for the sunset on the next range, miles and miles away.

CHAPTER THREE

Neville gazed at the wee yellow man hopelessly, and the wee yellow man gazed at Neville, and neither spoke a word until the man with the large ears was well out of the way. Then the Last Sunbeam grew quite cheerful again.

"Well," said he, "you heard what the head scene-shifter said. You certainly can't go home by the way you came. The only thing for you to do is to go round. You'll just about have time to do it, if you hurry."

"Go round?" repeated Neville in a puzzled voice. "Go round what, round where?"

"Round the world, of course," replied the little yellow man.

"Round the world?" cried Neville. "Why you must be making fun of me, and I think that is very unkind."

"Not a bit of it," laughed the little yellow man. "You need not make such as fuss about it. Why, I go round the world once every day with the sunset. You have only to go a bit faster so as to do it in a few minutes, and with the Cloud Horse to help you that's easily managed. Don't you worry about the Cloud Horse. He has got to do just whatever I tell him. Now, excuse me for one moment and I'll give you full directions."

With that the wee yellow man went behind a pink cloud and came back with a beautiful blue flower in his hand.

"This," he said, handing the flower to Neville, "is a Sky Flower. It is made entirely out of a genuine piece of sky, and it is a talisman—that's a longer word for charm, you know— which takes you free round the world. The one thing you have to

54

remember is that you mustn't, on any account, lose that flower until you get home again. Now, just exactly what you have to do is to travel West and race round the world until you catch up with this evening again. It is quite simple."

"Simple!" cried Neville. "Why I don't understand it at all."

"Dear me!" said the wee yellow man rather impatiently, "you are very dense. Now listen carefully. The world, you know, turns round from West to East, and that makes it seem as if the sun is going round the world from East to West. Very well. So what you have to do is to ride West upon the Cloud horse much faster than the sun appears to travel, and catch him up again before he gets well away from here. The Cloud horse is in good condition, and you should easily do it in a few minutes."

"A few minutes!" gasped Neville.

"Keep quiet and listen," snapped the wee yellow man. "A few miles West from here you will come into broad daylight. That will be afternoon. After that you will meet mid-day, and, passing that, you will reach the place where it is only dawn. That's about half-way round the earth. Show the Sky Flower to the porter of the Dawn, and he will let you through. Then you get to the half of the world where it is night, and you must race round that till you reach the place where it is only evening. That will be THIS evening, somewhere about here, for you will have taken only a few minutes altogether. And when you see your own home or the bald hill again, grasp the Sky Flower tightly in your hand, jump off the Cloud horse, and you will float gracefully down to the earth. It won't hurt you. Then you can go home, and I hope you will not be late for dinner."

"But," began Neville, "I can't understand—"

"My time is valuable," said the wee yellow man, as he shook hands. "Good-bye, and a pleasant journey." With that he smacked the Cloud Horse smartly on the flank, and in a moment it was racing into the West at a most terrific pace.

Of course, now that aeroplanes have been invented, flying

is not thought so wonderful as once it was. But loafing along through the air in a biplane or a monoplane at eighty or a hundred miles an hour is a very tame business when you compare it with racing the day round the world on a Cloud horse. And Neville is very probably the only person who has ever done that yet.

Almost before he knew what had happened, he had left evening far behind and was riding in broad daylight. The cloud Horse had ridden high in the air, and Neville saw the broad country, with plains and hills and forest lands, stretched far beneath him. An instant later, and the land was no longer below him, but the wide sea, sparkling in brilliant sunlight.

Before he had time to notice very much he had reached midday, high over a strange foreign land, and was racing through the morning toward the dawn. So quickly did he go that there was little chance of seeing anything clearly; but he had glimpses of many strange sights. Many ships he saw upon the sea—small ships and stately steamers crawling over the ocean like strange water-beetles. Once, as the Cloud Horse drifted low, Neville saw a beautiful sailing-ship, with all sails set, and strange-looking men upon the deck. They looked very like pirates, and perhaps they were; but Neville had no time to make sure, for the very next minute he was over a wild land where he saw a horde of black men, with spears and clubs, hunting an elephant through a clearing in a great jungle. As he looked, the elephant turned to charge the hunters; but what happened then Neville did not see, for in a moment more he was above a great city with crowds of people in the streets—people dressed in strange, bright-coloured clothes—and there were bells ringing and whistles blowing. Then a great desert spread beneath him, with no living thing in sight but a great tawny lion prowling over the sand. Then came the sea again, and more ships; and the light began to grow dim, for he was nearly half-way round the earth, and was approaching the dawn.

Dimmer grew the light, and dimmer yet, just as though evening were coming—and before him, Neville saw the dawn like a silvery gateway in the sky. Straight toward it the Cloud Horse rushed, and stopped so suddenly that Neville almost fell off.

"What's all this? What's all this?" cried a small voice; and Neville saw beside the silver gateway, a little man dressed from top to toe in silver grey. It was the Porter of the Dawn, sometimes called the First Sunbeam.

Before Neville could answer, the little grey man had caught sight of the Sky Flower.

"Ah, you have the talisman," said he. "Pass in! and don't stop to gossip, because I'm very busy this morning. A pleasant journey," he added as he smacked the cloud horse on the shoulder; and in an instant Neville had passed through the dawn and plunged into the night.

It was a dark night, with no moon, for the sky was overcast with dense clouds. Above these the Cloud horse flew, and overhead Neville saw the rushing stars, and below only the blackness of heavy clouds. But more often the Cloud horse flew low, and then there was little to be seen. By the lights of moving ships Neville knew that sometimes he was above the sea. Sometimes twinkling lights in towns or solitary farms, or the sudden blaze of a great city told him that the land was beneath him. Once, through the blackness, he saw a great forest fire upon an island, and the light of it lit up the sea, and showed the natives crowded upon the beach and in the shallows, and some making off in canoes.

Then darkness swallowed the Cloud Horse again, and the blazing island was left far behind.

After that, Neville began to feel a little drowsy. Perhaps he did sleep a little, for the next thing he saw was a faint light in the sky before him, as though the dawn were coming. But he knew it must be the evening, because he was coming back to the place from which he had started, and was catching up with the sun. You see, he had only been gone a few minutes.

The Cloud Horse flew very low now; and rapidly the darkness grew less. Then, long before he expected it, Neville saw the roof of his own home below him. He could see the garden in the twilight and his own dog sniffing about among the trees as though in search of him.

Neville began to think about jumping now, and he was rather nervous. He might land softly and he might not. He only had the wee yellow man's word for that.

Then, to his horror, he saw that they had passed his home and were over the bald hill. There was no time to lose. The Cloud Horse was taking him into the sunset again, and, if he did, what would the head scene-shifter say then?

So, grasping the Sky Flower very tightly, Neville closed his eyes and jumped. He half expected to fall quickly and be dashed to pieces upon the earth; but, instead, he floated in the air like a feather, swaying and drifting, and slowly sinking all the time towards the ground. It was a very pleasant sensation indeed.

The bald hill was beneath him as he came slowly down, down, down.

He could see the Cloud Horse—now little more than a small white speck—rushing on to catch the sunset. And still he sank down ever so slowly towards the top of the bald hill.

His little dog had caught sight of him now, and came rushing out the gate and up the bald hill, barking loudly. And he kept on sinking nearer to the earth, down, down, nearer and nearer—and then, quite suddenly, he seemed to forget everything.

The next thing Neville remembered was feeling something wet and warm upon his cheek. He opened his eyes and saw that the little dog was licking his face. Sitting up, he looked about him. He was in the grass on the top of the bald hill; night was very near, and the first star was just beginning to twinkle.

Then, quite suddenly, Neville remembered the Cloud horse and the little yellow man and the little silver man and the head scene-shifter and the wonderful journey and all the rest of it.

"Well, what a remarkable dream," said Neville, stretching his arms. And, as he did so, the Sky Flower fell from his hand.

So it was not a dream after all; for, if it was, how could he explain that Sky Flower? He picked it up and carried it very tenderly, as he set off home to dinner, his little dog trotting at his heels.

"What a beautiful flower!" said Neville's mother when he got home. "Where ever did you get it?"

"It is a piece of the genuine sky," said Neville proudly, as he gave it to her.

His mother smiled at him as she said, "That is a very nice thing to say, and it certainly does look like a little piece of the sky. But, of course, it couldn't possibly be a real piece."

Then Neville knew that if he were to tell the story of his wonderful ride, and tried to explain that he had been right around the world since he went out to play, his parents would find it very, very hard to believe. So he said nothing, but ate a very good dinner.

But Neville's mother put the flower in a vase upon the mantel; and to this day it is still there, as fresh and bright as ever. It will not fade. Neville's mother thinks that is a very strange and wonderful thing. And so it is.

Since that day, when Neville goes to the top of the bald hill to watch a sunset, he is almost sure that, just as the golden light is fading, he can see a little yellow man by the gateway; and it seems to him that the little yellow man waves a cheery greeting. But, whether this is so or not, Neville always waves back; and he feels very happy to think that he has a good friend inside the sunset.

THE TRAM-MAN

I'd like to be a Tram-man, and ride about all day,
Calling out, "Fares, please!" in quite a 'ficious way,
With pockets full of pennies which I'd make the people pay.
But in the hottest days I'd take my tram down to the Bay;
And when I saw the nice cool sea I'd shout "Hip, hip, hooray!"
But I wouldn't be a Tram-man if....
I couldn't stop and play.

Would you?

THE AXE-MAN

High on the hills, where the tall trees grow,
There lives an axeman that I know.
From his little hut by a ferny creek,
Day after day, week after week,
He goes each morn with his shining axe,
Trudging along by the forest tracks;
And he chops and he chops till the daylight goes—
High on the hills, where the blue-gum grows.

(Chip!.. Chop!.. Chip!.. Chop!)
There's a log to move and a branch to lop.
Now to the felling! His sharp axe bites
Into a tree on the forest heights,
And scarce for a breath does the axeman stop—
(Chip!.. Chop!.. Chip!.. Chop!)
Bell-birds watch him; and in the fern
Wallabies listen awhile, and turn
Back through the bracken, and off they hop.
(Chip!.. Chop!.. Chip!.. Chop!)
Patient and tireless, blow on blow
The axeman swings as the minutes go;
While the echoes ring from the mountain-top.
(Chip!.. Chop!.. Chip!.. Chop!)

Round about him the rabbits play,
Skipping and scampering all the day,
And the sweet young grass by the logs they crop.
(Chip!.. Chop!.. Chip!.. Chop!)

Crimson parrots above him climb,
Chattering, chattering all the time,

As down from the branches the twigs they drop.
(Chip!.. Chop!.. Chip! Chop!)
Steadily, surely, on he goes,
Shaking the tree with his mighty blows:
There's never a pause and there's never a stop.
(Chip!.. Chop!.. Chip!.. Chop!)

Out from the bush beyond is heard
The swaggering song of the butcher-bird
Seeking a joint for his butcher's shop.
(Chip!.. Chop!.. Chip!.. Chop!)
Deeper and deeper the cut creeps in,
While the parrots shriek with a deafening din,
And the chips fly out with a flip and a flop.
(Chip! Chop! Chip! Chop!)
Yellow robins come flocking round,
Watching the chips as they fall to ground,
Darting to catch the grubs that drop.
(Chip!.. Chop!.. Chip!.. Chop!)

The blows come quicker. The axe-blade hums,
Stand well back, there, before she comes!
Hark! How the splinters crack and pop—
(Chip!.. Chop!.. Chip!.. Chop!)
Listen! Listen! She's creaking now!
Look, high up, at that trembling bough!
Another second, and down she'll smash,
Shaking the earth with a mighty crash;
Look at her! Look at her! (Chip! Chop!
Chip!........Chip!)
        Wee—E—E—E—E—E—-

FLOP!

THE DROVERS

Out across the spinifex, out across the sand,
Out across the saltbush to Never Never Land
  That's the way the drovers go, jogging down the track—
  That's the way the drovers go. But how do they come back?
Back across the saltbush from Never Never Land.
Back across the spinifex, back across the sand.

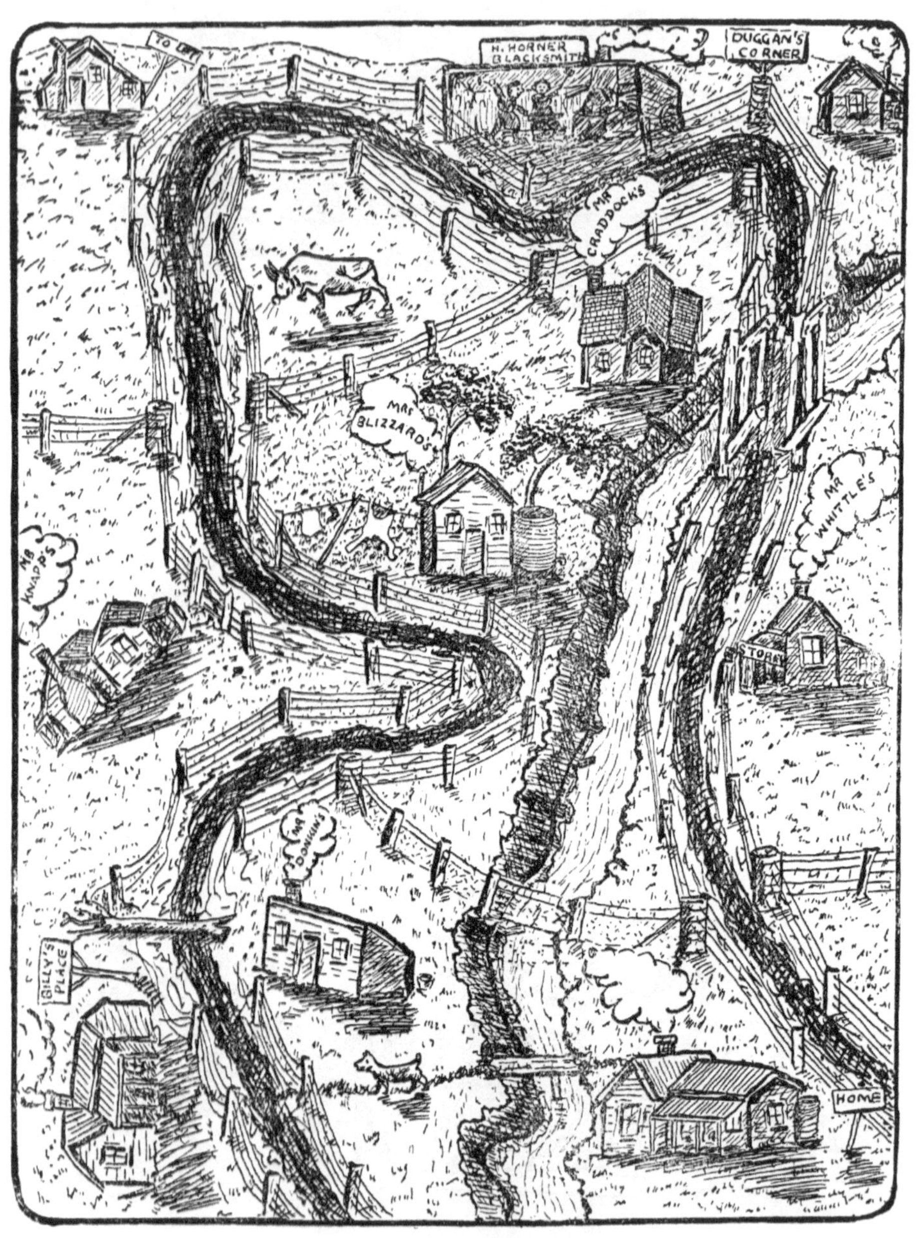

THE LONG ROAD HOME

THE LONG ROAD HOME

When I go back from Billy's place I always have to roam
The mazy road, the crazy road that leads the long way home.
Ma always says, "Why don't you come through Mr Donkin's land?
The footbridge track will bring you back." Ma doesn't understand.
I cannot go that way, you know, because of Donkin's dog;
So I set forth and travel north, and cross the fallen log.

Last week, when I was coming by, that log had lizards in it;
And you can't say I stop to play if I just search a minute.
I look around upon the ground and, if there are no lizards,
I go right on and reach the turn in front of Mrs Blizzard's.
I do not seek to cross the creek, because it's deep and floody,
And Ma would be annoyed with me if I came home all muddy.

Perhaps I throw a stone or so at Mrs Blizzard's tank,
Because it's great when I aim straight to hear the stone go "Plank!"
Then west I wend from Blizzard's Bend, and not a moment wait,
Except, perhaps, at Mr Knapp's, to swing upon his gate.
So up the hill I go, until I reach the little paddock
That Mr Jones at present owns and rents to Mr Craddock.

For boys my size the sudden rise is quite a heavy pull,
And yet I fear a short-cut here because of Craddock's bull;
So I just tease the bull till he's as mad as he can get,
And then I face the corner place that's been so long to let.
It's very well for Ma to tell about my dawdling habits.
What would you do, suppose you knew the place was thick
    with rabbits?

I do not stay for half a day, as Ma declares I do.
No, not for more than half-an-hour—perhaps an hour—or two.
Then down the drop I run, slip-slop, where all the road is slithy.
And have to go quite close, you know, to Mr Horner's smithy.

A moment I might tarry by the fence to watch them hammer,
And, I must say, learn more that way than doing sums and
    grammar.

And, if I do sometimes climb through, I do not mean to linger.
Though I did stay awhile the day Bill Horner burst his finger.
I just stand there to see the pair bang some hot iron thing
And watch Bill Horner swing the sledge and hit the anvil—Bing!
(For Mr Horner and his son are great big brawny fellows:
Both splendid chaps!) And then, perhaps, they let me blow the
    bellows.

A while I stop beside the shop, and talk to Mr Horner;
Then off I run, and race like fun around by Duggan's Corner.
It's getting late, and I don't wait beside the creek a minute,
Except to stop, maybe, and drop a few old pebbles in it.
A few yards more, and here's the store that's kept by Mr
    Whittle—
And you can't say I waste the day if I 'ust wait... a little.

One day, you know, a year ago, a man gave me a penny,
And Mr Whittle sold me sweets (but not so very many).
You never know your luck, and so I look to see what's new
In Mr Whittle's window. There's a peppermint or two,
Some buttons and tobacco (Mr Whittle calls it "baccy"),
And fish in tins, and tape, and pins.... And then a voice calls,
    "Jacky!"

"I'm coming, Ma. I've been so far-around by Duggan's Corner.
I had to stay awhile to say 'Good day' to Mr Horner.
I feel so fagged; I've tramped and dragged through mud and over
    logs, Ma—
I could not go short-cuts, you know, because of bulls and dogs,
    Ma.
The creek, Ma? Why, it's very high! You don't call that a gutter?
Bill Horner chews tobacco, Ma.... I'd like some bread and butter."

THE BAND

Hey, there! Listen awhile! Listen awhile, and come.
Down in the street there are marching feet, and I hear the
  beat of a drum.
Bim! Boom!! Out of the room! Pick up your hat and fly!
Isn't it grand? The band! The band! The band is marching by!

Oh, the clarinet is the finest yet, and the uniforms are gay.
  Tah, rah! We don't go home—
  Oom, pah! We won't go home—
Oh, we shan't go home, and we can't go home when the band
  begins to play.

Oh, see them swinging along, swinging along the street!
Left, right! buttons so bright, jackets and caps so neat.
Ho, the Fire Brigade, or a dress parade of the Soldier-men is
   grand;
But everyone, for regular fun, wants a Big-Brass-Band.

The slide-trombone is a joy alone, and the drummer! He's a
   treat!
   So, Rackety-rumph! We don't go home—
   Boom, Bumph! We won't go home—
Oh, we shan't go home, and we can't go home while the band
   is in the street.
   Tooral-ooral, Oom-pah!

                  The band is in the street!

BESSIE AND THE BUNYIP

Bessie met a bunyip down along the track,
In his hand a billy and a swag upon his back.
  And you will hardly believe it, but when Bessie
      shouted,"Shoo!"
He turned a double somersault and went quite blue.

GOOD ENOUGH

I do not think there ever was,
  Or ever will, or ever could be,
A little girl or little boy
  As good as she or as he should be.

But still, I think, you will agree,
  Though perfect very, very few are,
They're not so bad when "pretty good"—
  That's just about as good as you are.

THE PORTER

I'd like to be a porter, and always on the run,
Calling out, "Stand aside!" and asking leave of none.
Shoving trucks on people's toes, and having splendid fun,
Slamming all the carriage doors and locking every one—
And, when they asked to be let in, I'd say, "It can't be done."
    But I wouldn't be a porter if...
        The luggage weighed a ton.

            Would you?

GROWING UP

Little Tommy Tadpole began to weep and wail,
For little Tommy Tadpole had lost his little tail;
And his mother didn't know him as he wept upon a log,
For he wasn't Tommy Tadpole, but Mr. Thomas Frog.

THE UNSOCIABLE WALLABY

Willie spied a wallaby hopping through the fern—
Here a jump, here a thump, there a sudden turn.
  Willie called the wallaby, begging him to stop,
  But he went among the wattles with a
                flip,
                      flap,
                            flop!

* * *

I wonder whether, all together, you and I and father
Could eat a bun that weighs a ton. I'd like to try it, rather.

I want to know why roosters crow at dawning of the day.
Is it because they cannot think of something else to say?

* * *

THE SONG OF THE SULKY STOCKMAN

Come, let us sing with a right good ring
   (Sing hey for lifting lay, sing hey!)
Of any old, sunny old, silly old thing.
   (Sing ho for the ballad of a backblock day!)
The sun shone brightly overhead,
And the shearers stood by the shearing shed;
But "The run wants rain," the stockman said
(Sing di-dum, wattle-gum, Narrabori Ned.
   For a lifting lay sing hey!)

The colts were clipped and the sheep were shorn
   (Sing hey for a lilting lay, sing hey!)
But the stockman stood there all forlorn.
   (Sing ho for the ballad of a backblock day!)
The rails were up and the gate was tied,
And the big black bull was safe inside;
But "The wind's gone West!" the stockman sighed
(Sing, di-dum, wattle-gum, rally for a ride.
   For a lifting lay sing hey!)

The cook came out as the clock struck one
   (Sing hey for a lilting lay, sing hey!)
And the boundary rider got his gun.
   (Sing ho for the ballad of a backblock day!)
He fired it once at an old black crow;
But the shot went wide, for he aimed too low;
And the stockman said, "Fat stock is low."
(Sing, di-dum, wattle-gum, Jerridiiii Joe.
   For a lifting lay sing hey!)

They spread their swags in the gum-tree's shade
   (Sing hey for a lilting lay, sing hey!)
For the work was done and the cheques were paid.
   (Sing ho for the ballad of a backblock day!)

The overseer rode in at three,
But his horse pulled back and would not gee,
And the stockman said, "We're up a tree!"
(Sing, di-dum, wattle-gum, Johnny-cake for tea.
    For a lilting lay sing hey!)

The sun sank down and the stars shone out
    (Sing hey for a lifting lay, sing hey!)
And the old book-keeper moped about.
    (Sing ho for the ballad of a backblock day!)
The dingo wailed to the mopoke's call,
The crazy colt stamped in his stall;
But the stockman groaned, "it's bunk for all."
(Sing, di-dum, wattle-gum, wattle-gum, wattle-gum,
    Hey for a backblock day!
            Sing hey!
    Sing hey for a lifting lay!)

OUR COW

Down by the sliprails stands our cow
    Chewing, chewing, chewing,
She does not care what folks out there
    In the great, big world are doing.
She sees the small cloud-shadows pass
    And green grass shining under.
If she does think, what does she think
    About it all, I wonder?

She sees the swallows skimming by
    Above the sweet young clover,
The light reeds swaying in the wind
    And tall trees bending over.
Far down the track she hears the crack
    of bullock-whips, and raving
Of angry men where, in the sun,
    Her fellow-beasts are slaving.

Girls, we are told, can scratch and scold,
    And boys will fight and wrangle,
And big, grown men, just now and then,
    Fret o'er some fingle-fangle,
Vexing the earth with grief or mirth,
    Longing, rejoicing, rueing—
But by the sliprails stands our cow,
    Chewing.

THE TEACHER

I'd like to be a teacher, and have a clever brain,
Calling out, "Attention, please!" and "Must I speak in vain?"
I'd be quite strict with boys and girls whose minds I had to train,
And all the books and maps and things I'd carefully explain;
I'd make then learn the dates of kings, and all the capes of Spain;
But I wouldn't be a teacher if...
I couldn't use the cane.

Would you?

THE SPOTTED HEIFERS

Mr Jeremiah Jeffers
Owned a pair of spotted heifers
These he sold for two pounds ten
To Mr Robert Raymond Wren

Who reared them in the lucerne paddocks
Owned by Mr Martin Maddox,
And sold them, when they grew to cows,
To Mr Donald David Dowse.

A grazier, Mr Egbert Innes,
Bought them then for twenty guineas,
Milked the cows, and sold the milk
To Mr Stephen Evan Silk.

Who rents a butter factory
From Mr Laurence Lampard-Lee.
Here, once a week, come for his butter
The grocer, Mr Roland Rutter,

Who keeps a shop in Sunny Street
Next door to Mr Peter Peat.
He every afternoon at two
Sent his fair daughter, Lucy Loo,

To Mr Rutter's shop to buy
Such things as were not priced too high,
Especially a shilling tin
Of "Fuller's Food for Folk Too Thin."

This food was bought for Lucy Loo—
A girl of charming manners, who

Was much too pale and much too slight
To be a very pleasant sight.

When Lucy Loo beheld the butter
Stocked by Mr Roland Rutter,
She said, "I'll have a pound of that."
She had it, and thenceforth grew fat.

We now go back to Mr Jeffers,
Who sold the pair of spotted heifers.
He had a son, James Edgar John,
A handsome lad to gaze upon,

Who had now reached that time of life
When young men feel they need a wife;
But no young girl about the place
Exactly had the kind of face

That seemed to suit James Edgar John—
A saddening thing to think upon,
For he grew sad and sick of life
Because he could not find a wife.

One day young James was passing by
(A look of sorrow in his eye)
The shop of Mr Roland Rutter,
When Lucy Loo came out with butter.

At once James Edgar John said, "That
Is just the girl for me! She's fat."
He offered her his heart and hand
And prospects of his father's land.

The Reverend Saul Sylvester Slight
Performed the simple marriage rite.
The happy couple went their way,
And lived and loved unto this day.

Events cannot be far foreseen;
And all ths joy might not have been
If Mr Jeremiah Jeffers
Had kept his pair of spotted heifers.

TEA TALK

'Excuse me if I sit on you,' the cup said to the saucer.
  'I fear I've been here all the afternoon.'
'Spare excuses,' said the saucer; 'you have sat on me
    before, sir.'
  'Oh, I'll stir him up directly,' said the spoon.
'Stop your clatter! Stop your clatter!' cried the bread-
    and-butter platter
  'Tittle-tattle!' sneered the tea-pot, with a shrug;
'Now, the most important question is my chronic
    indigestion.'
  'Ah, you've taken too much tannin,' jeered the jug.
'Hey, hey, hey!' sang the silver-plated tray,
'It's time you had your faces washed. I've come to clear
    away!'

THE LOOKING-GLASS

When I look into the looking glass
    I'm always sure to see—
No matter how I dodge about—
    Me, looking out at me.

I often wonder as I look,
    And those strange features spy,
If I, in there, think I'm as plain
    As I, out here, think I.

WOOLLOOMOOLOO

Here's a ridiculous riddle for you:
How many o's are there in Woolloomooloo?
    Two for the W, two for the m,
    Four for the l's, and that's plenty for them.

* * *

I wonder what the Jacks have got to laugh and laugh about
I'm sure the worms don't see the joke when Jacky digs them out.

I wonder which is best: a rich plum-pudding stuffed with
    plums,
Or lemon ice, or plain boiled rice, or long-division sums.

* * *

THE BARBER

I'd like to be a barber, and learn to shave and clip,
Calling out, "Next please!" and pocketing my tip.
All day I'd hear my scissors going, "Snip, Snip, Snip;"
I'd lather people's faces, and their noses I would grip
While I shaved most carefully along the upper lip.
   But I wouldn't be a barber if...
      The razor was to slip.

         Would you?

OLD FARMER JACK

Old farmer Jack gazed on his wheat,
    And feared the frost would nip it.
Said he, "it's nearly seven feet—
    I must begin to strip it."

He stripped it with a stripper and
    He bagged it with a bagger;
The bags were all so lumpy that
    They made the lumper stagger.

The lumper staggered up the stack
    Where he was told to stack it;
And Jack was paid and put the cash
    Inside his linen jacket.

OLD BLACK JACKO

Old Black Jacko
    Smokes tobacco
    In his little pipe of clay.
Puff, puff, puff,
He never has enough
    Though he smokes it all day.

But his lubra says, "Mine tink dat Jacky
Him shmoke plenty too much baccy."

BIRD SONG

I detest the Carrion Crow!
(He's a raven, don't you know?)
    He's a greedy glutton, also, and a ghoul,
And his sanctimonious caw
Rubs my temper on the raw.
    He's a demon, and a most degraded fowl.

I admire the pert Blue-wren
And his dainty little hen—
    Though she hasn't got a trace of blue upon her;
But she's pleasing, and she's pretty,
    And she sings a cheerful ditty;
While her husband is a gentleman of honour.

I despise the Pallid Cuckoo,
A disreputable "crook" who
    Shirks her duties for a lazy life of ease.
I abhor her mournful call,
Which is not a song at all
    But a cross between a whimper and a wheeze.

THE SAILOR

I'd like to be a sailor—a sailor bold and bluff—
Calling out, "Ship ahoy!" in manly tones and gruff.
I'd learn to box the compass, and to reef and tack and luff;
I'd sniff and sniff the briny breeze and never get enough.
Perhaps I'd chew tobacco, or an old black pipe I'd puff,
  But I wouldn't be a sailor if...
  The sea was very rough.

Would you?

THE FAMINE

Cackle and lay, cackle and lay!
How many eggs did you get to-day?
    None in the manger, and none in the shed,
    None in the box where the chickens are fed,
    None in the tussocks and none in the tub,
    And only a little one out in the scrub.
Oh, I say! Dumplings to-day.
I fear that the hens must be laying away.

THE FEAST

Cackle and lay, cackle and lay!
How many eggs did you get to-day?
    Two in the manger, and four in the shed,
    Six in the box where the chickens are fed,
    Two in the tussocks and ten in the tub,
    And nearly two dozen right out in the scrub.
Hip, hooray! Pudding to-day!
I think that the hens are beginning to lay.

UPON THE ROAD TO ROCKABOUT

Upon the road to Rockabout
   I came upon some sheep—
A large and woolly flock about
   As wide as it was deep.

I was about to turn about
   To ask the man to tell
Some things I wished to learn about
   Both sheep and wool as well,

When I beheld a rouseabout
   Who lay upon his back
Beside a little house about
   A furlong from the track.

I had a lot to talk about,
   And said to him "Good day."
But he got up to walk about,
   And so I went away—

A CHANGE OF AIR

Now, a man in Oodnadatta
He grew fat, and he grew fatter,
    Though he hardly had a thing to eat for dinner;
While a man in Booboorowie
Often sat and wondered how he
    Could prevent himself from growing any thinner.

So the man from Oodnadatta
    He came down to Booboorowie,
Where he rapidly grew flatter;
    And the folk will tell you how he
Urged the man from Booboorowie
    To go up to Oodnadatta—
Where he lived awhile, and now he
    Is considerably fatter.

POLLY DIBBS

Mrs Dibbs—Polly Dibbs,
    Standing at a tub,
Washing other people's clothes—
    Rub-Rub-Rub.
Poor, old, skinny arms
    White with soapy foam—
At night she takes her shabby hat
    And goes off home.

Mrs Dibbs—Polly Dibbs—
    Is not very rich.
She goes abroad all day to scrub,
    And home at night to stitch.
She wears her shabby hat awry,
    Perched on a silly comb;
And people laugh at Polly Dibbs
    As she goes home.

Mrs Dibbs—Mother Dibbs—
    Growing very old,
Says, "it's a hard world!"
    And sniffs and drats the cold.
She says it is a cruel world,
    A weary world to roam.
But God will smile on Polly Dibbs
    When she goes Home.

BIRD SONG

I suspect the Kookaburra,
For his methods are not thorough
    In his highly praised campaign against the snakes.
And the small birds, one and all,
Curse him for a cannibal—
    Though he certainly is cheerful when he wakes.

LULLABY

You are much too big to dandle,
And I will not leave the candle.
    Go to sleep.
You are growing naughty, rather,
And I'll have to speak to father.
    Go to sleep!
If you're good I shall not tell, then.
Oh, a story? Very well, then.
    Once upon a time, a king, named Crawley Creep,
Had a very lovely daughter....
You don't want a drink of water!
    Go to sleep! *There! There!* Go to sleep.

I WONDER

I wonder why I wear a tie. It is not warm to wear;
But if I left it off someone would say it was not there.

I wonder, if I took a whiff of father's pipe for fun,
Would I be big and strong like him, or just his small, sick son?

I wonder when our old white hen will know her squawk
    betrays her.
I think she lets us find her eggs just so that we shall praise her.

THE PUBLISHER

I'd like to be a publisher, And publish massive tomes
Written in a massive style by blokes with massive domes—
Science books, and histories of Egypt's day and Rome's,
Books of psycho-surgery to mine the minds of momes,
And solemn pseudo-psychic stuff to tell where Topsy roams
When her poor clay is put away beneath the spreading holms;
Books about electrocuting little seeds with ohms
To sternly show them how to grow in sands, and clays, and loams,
And bravely burst infinitives, like angry agronomes;
Books on breeding aeroplanes and airing aerodromes,
On bees that buzz in bonnets and the kind that build the combs,
Made plain with pretty pictures done in crimsons, mauves,
    and chromes;
And diagrams to baulk the brain of Mr. Sherlock Holmes.
I'd set the scientists to work like superheated gnomes,
And make them write and write and write until the printer foams
And lino men, made "loony", go to psychopathic homes.
I'd publish books, I would—large books on ants and antinomes
And palimpsests and palinodes and pallid pallindromes:
    But I wouldn't be a publisher if....
            I got many "pomes."
                    Would you?

91

GOOD NIGHT

And so, Good Night. I'm rather tired.
I hardly thought I'd be required
  To draw a lot of pictures, too,
  When I arranged to write for you.
I found it hard, but did my best;
And now I need a little rest.
  If you are pleased, why, that's all right.
  I'm rather tired. And so

This very charming gentleman,
    extremely old and gruff,
He slowly shook his head and took a
    great big pinch of snuff,
Then he spluttered and he muttered and
    he loudly shouted "Fie!
To tear your books is wicked sir! and
    likewise all my eye!"
I don't know what he meant by that. He
    had such piercing eyes.
And, he said,
    "Mark—ME—boy!
    Books will
    make you wise."

This very charming gentleman said,
    "Hum," and "Hoity, Toit!
A book is not a building block, a
    cushion or a quoit.
Soil your books and spoil your books?
    Is that the thing to do?
Gammon, sir! and Spinach, sir! And
    Fiddle-faddle, too!"
He blinked so quick, and thumped his
    stick, then gave me such a stare.
And he said, "Mark—ME—boy!
    Books—need—CARE!"